Herd of Cows! Flock of Sheep!

Quiet! I'm Tired! I Need My Sleep!

First Edition
06 05 04 03 02   5 4 3 2 1

Text © 2002 by Rick Walton
Illustrations © 2002 by Julie Olson

Published by
Gibbs Smith, Publisher
P.O. Box 667
Layton, Utah 84041

OCT 2 1 2002

Orders: (1-800) 748-5439
www.gibbs-smith.com

Edited by Suzanne Gibbs Taylor
Designed and produced by FORTHGEAR, Inc.
Printed and bound in Hong Kong

Library of Congress Cataloging-in-Publication Data

Walton, Rick.
  Herd of cows! Flock of sheep! Quiet! I'm tired! I need my sleep! /
Rick Walton ; illustrated by Julie Hansen Olson.
     p. cm.
Summary: Farmer Brown has just finished harvesting his crops before the rains come and wants nothing more than to sleep, but groups of all kinds of animals, birds, insects and fish insist on disturbing him.
  ISBN 1-58685-153-5
 [1. Farmers—Fiction. 2. Sleep—Fiction. 3. Animals—Fiction. 4. English language—Collective nouns—Fiction. 5. Animal sounds—Fiction.] I. Olson, Julie, 1976- ill. II. Title.
  PZ7.W1774 He 2002
  [E]—dc21
                          2001006794

Herd of Cows! Flock of Sheep!

Quiet! I'm Tired! I Need My Sleep!

Rick Walton

**Illustrated by
Julie Olson**

Gibbs Smith, Publisher
Salt Lake City

To Bill and Wilma Walton,
and their army of kids and grandkids

—RW

To my little animals,
Jacob and Spencer

—JHO

The rain would be coming soon. So Farmer Bob worked day and night and day and night to harvest his crops. A little rain would be good for his plants. But too much could destroy them. And Farmer Bob guessed there might be too much rain.

Finally the corn, the potatoes, the beans, the tomatoes—all were safe in the barn, stored up high where they'd stay dry. He'd take them to market later.

But first, he had something important to do.

Sleep.

He trudged into his little house by the river, took off his boots, put on his pajamas and his sleep mask and dropped into bed. He was so tired. He hadn't slept in days . . . zzzzzz.

Farmer Bob had guessed right. That night, the rain came—a lot of it. It made the river rise. It rose slowly up the steps and into Farmer Bob's house.

It rose so high that it pushed open the double doors in Farmer Bob's bedroom, picked up his bed, and floated it right outside.

And Farmer Bob didn't notice a thing, because he was sooooo tired, and sooooo sound asleep.

In the morning, far downriver from Farmer Bob's house,
a flock of sheep grazed.

One looked up from his chewing and saw a most
unusual sight. "BAA!" she said.

The other sheep looked. "BAA, BAA, BAA, BAA!" They ran to
the river and called out to Farmer Bob, "BAA, BAA, BAA!"

Farmer Bob stirred, but he was still so tired.
Half asleep, he shouted,

"FLOCK OF SHEEP!
QUIET! I'M TIRED!
I NEED MY SLEEP!"

A herd of cows heard the sheep and came to see what was
happening. They joined the sheep in trying to warn Farmer Bob.

"MOO, MOO, MOO!
BAA! MOO!
BAA, BAA! MOO!"

Farmer Bob hollered back,
"HERD OF COWS!
FLOCK OF SHEEP!
QUIET! I'M TIRED!
I NEED MY SLEEP!"

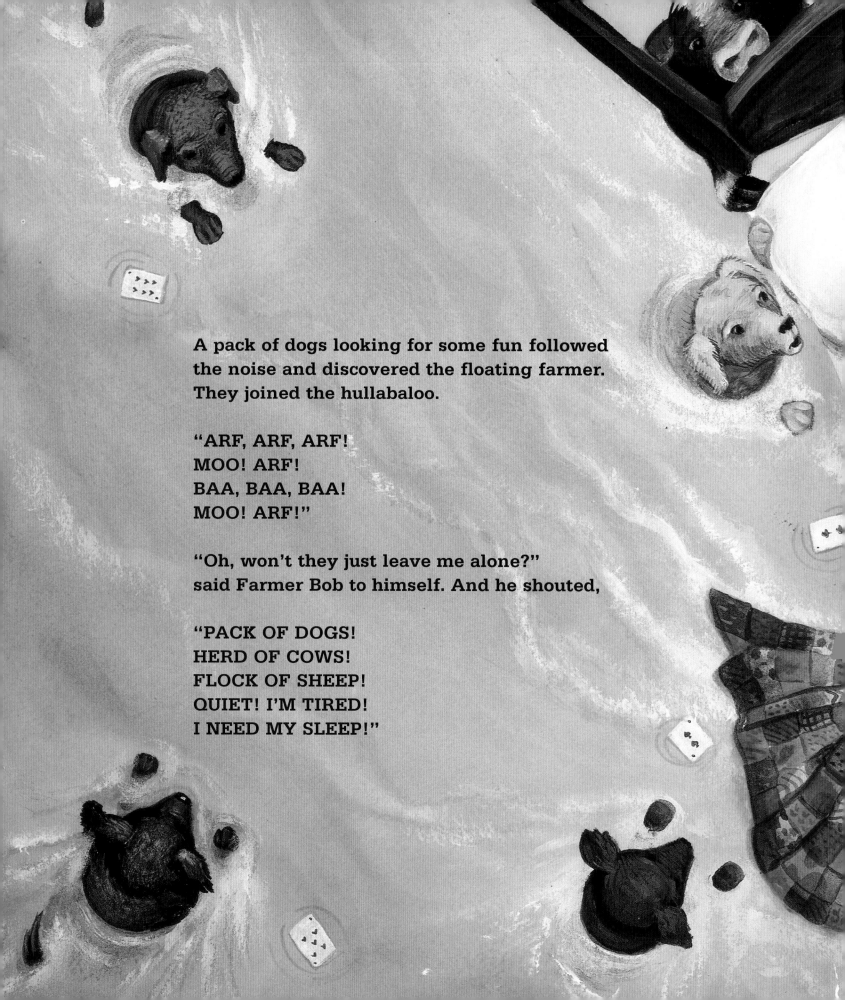

A pack of dogs looking for some fun followed
the noise and discovered the floating farmer.
They joined the hullabaloo.

"ARF, ARF, ARF!
MOO! ARF!
BAA, BAA, BAA!
MOO! ARF!"

"Oh, won't they just leave me alone?"
said Farmer Bob to himself. And he shouted,

"PACK OF DOGS!
HERD OF COWS!
FLOCK OF SHEEP!
QUIET! I'M TIRED!
I NEED MY SLEEP!"

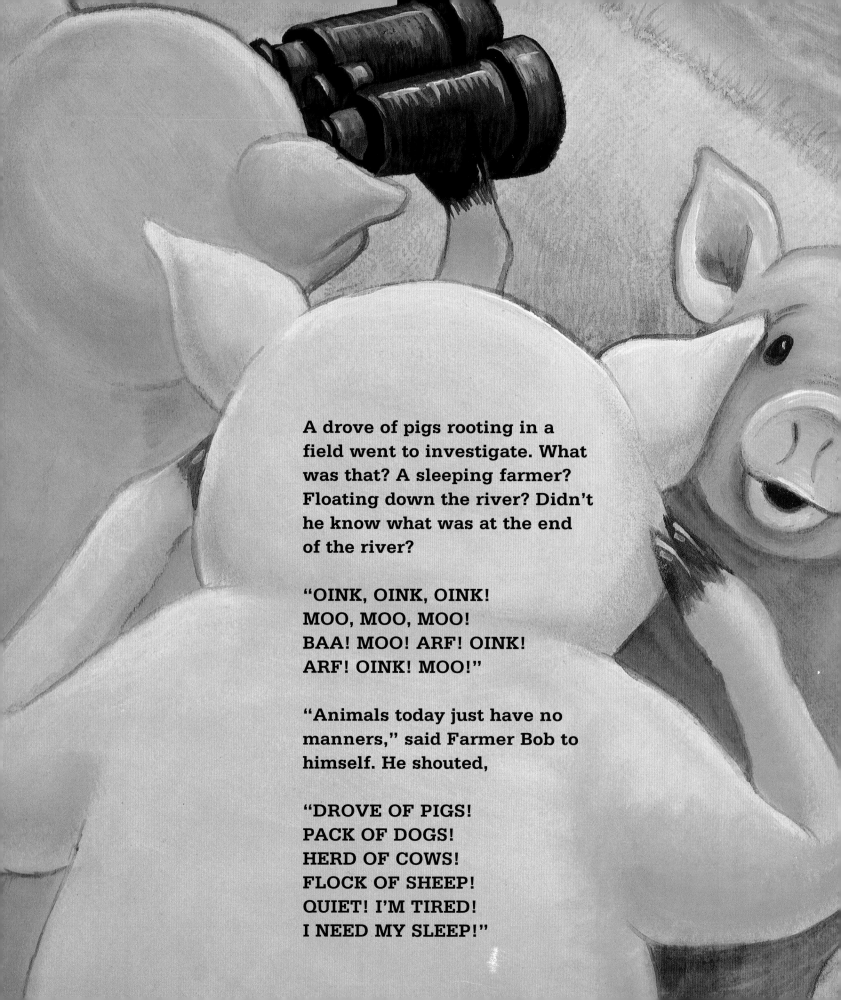

A drove of pigs rooting in a field went to investigate. What was that? A sleeping farmer? Floating down the river? Didn't he know what was at the end of the river?

"OINK, OINK, OINK!
MOO, MOO, MOO!
BAA! MOO! ARF! OINK!
ARF! OINK! MOO!"

"Animals today just have no manners," said Farmer Bob to himself. He shouted,

"DROVE OF PIGS!
PACK OF DOGS!
HERD OF COWS!
FLOCK OF SHEEP!
QUIET! I'M TIRED!
I NEED MY SLEEP!"

An army of frogs hunting flies by the river saw
Farmer Bob. Oh, no! He was floating toward . . .

"RIBET, RIBET! MOO, MOO!
OINK! ARF! BAA! MOO!
RIBET, RIBET! MOO! BAA! ARF!"

"How rude," said Farmer Bob.

"ARMY OF FROGS!
DROVE OF PIGS!
PACK OF DOGS!
HERD OF COWS!
FLOCK OF SHEEP!
QUIET! I'M TIRED!
I NEED MY SLEEP!"

The animals started to panic. The farmer was still floating, and there wasn't much time left. They sent out a general, all-purpose, "come quick, it's an emergency" alarm. And they were quickly joined by creatures of all kinds.

The pigs outlined a plan.
And everyone sprang into action.

A colony of beavers raced downriver and began chewing down trees. SPLASH! Into the river the trees fell. A school of fish tried to push them together into a dam.

But it wasn't working. The trees just floated away too quickly.

So much for Plan A.

The pigs quickly outlined Plan B.

A nest of mice brought their lifetime collection of rope and string . . . which a gaggle of geese carried to the bed and tied around the bedposts. Then the geese took the string in their bills and tried to fly.

But, no, the bed was too heavy to lift.

On to Plan C, and time was running out.

A cloud of gnats flew out to the farmer and up his nose, while a swarm of bees began to sting the farmer's toes.

Farmer Bob swatted and kicked. "Bothersome bugs," he muttered. "Must have left the window open."

The gnats and bees were not stopped. They kept flying up his nose. They kept stinging his toes.

Finally, Farmer Bob couldn't take it anymore. He flipped off his sleep mask, and shouted, "THAT'S ENOUGH! I'M GOING TO GET YOU PESTY . . . YIPES!"

Farmer Bob finally realized where he was. "HELP ME! HELP ME! I CAN'T SWIM!"

The rest of Plan C then kicked in. A herd of horses formed a line. A nest of snakes joined in.

The last snake crawled onto the bed, wrapped himself around Farmer Bob's leg, and . . .

. . . pulled him into the river.

"NEIGH! NEIGH! NEIGH!" said the horses as they pulled. The snakes tightened, and slowly, together, they dragged Farmer Bob from the river, just as . . .

. . . his bed went over the waterfall.

On the riverbank, while a clowder of cats kept him warm, and a rafter of turkeys fanned him dry, the pigs jumped on Farmer Bob's belly to push out all the river water.

"Thput, shput, COUGH, COUGH!" A gush of water came out of Farmer Bob's mouth. The pigs hopped off, and Farmer Bob sat up.

"Thank you! Thank you! You saved my life, you wonderful animals . . ."

". . . and bugs," he added when he saw the gnats and bees.

And to show his gratitude, after he'd
dried and cleaned his soggy house,
Farmer Bob issued an invitation:

"Nest of Mice!
Army of frogs!
Drove of pigs!
Pack of dogs!
Herd of cows!
Flock of sheep!
And other friends
Who found me asleep
And saved my life—
Bug, bird, and beast—
Come to my place
For a feast!"
(Oh, yes, school of fish,
you're invited too.)

And they all came. Farmer Bob got out his good set of china, and served stacks of pancakes, messes of grits, bunches of bananas, and all the corn and potatoes and beans and tomatoes his friends could eat.

DO NOT
DISTURB

And when they finally left,
full and happy,
Farmer Bob went out
and bought a new bed,
which he put in his new bedroom
—on the second floor—
and went to sleep.